James Whitcomb Riley

The flying islands of the night

James Whitcomb Riley

The flying islands of the night

ISBN/EAN: 9783744723138

Printed in Europe, USA, Canada, Australia, Japan

Cover: Foto ©Andreas Hilbeck / pixelio.de

More available books at **www.hansebooks.com**

THE FLYING ISLANDS

OF THE NIGHT

BY

JAMES WHITCOMB RILEY

"A thynge of wytchencref—an idle dreme."

INDIANAPOLIS
THE BOWEN-MERRILL CO.
1892

TO

MADISON CAWEIN

FOR the Song's sake; even so:
Humor it, and let it go
All untamed and wild of wing—
Leave it ever truanting.

    Be its flight elusive.—Lo,
    For the Song's sake—even so.
    Yield it but an ear as kind
    As thou perkest to the wind.

Who will name us what the seas
Have sung on for centuries?
For the Song's sake! Even so—
Sing, O Seas! and Breezes, blow!

    Sing! or Wave or Wind or Bird—
    Sing! nor ever afterward
    Clear thy meaning to us—No!—
    For the Song's sake. Even so.

THE FLYING ISLANDS OF THE NIGHT.

DRAMATIS PERSONÆ.

KRUNG,   King—*of the* Spirks.

CRESTILLOMEEM, *The* Queen—*Second Consort to* Krung.

SPRAIVOLL,   *The* Tune-Fool.

AMPHINE,   Prince—*Son of* Krung.

DWAINIE,   *A* Princess—*of the* Wunks.

JUCKLET,   *A* Dwarf—*of the* Spirks.

CREECH *and*
GRITCHFANG,   }   Nightmares.

Counselors, Courtiers, Heralds, etc., etc., etc.

ACT I.

SCENE—THE FLYING ISLANDS.

SCENE I. Spirkland. *Time, Moondawn. Interior of Court of* KRUNG. *A vast, pendant star burns dimly in the dome above the throne.* CRESTILLOMEEM *discovered languidly reclining at foot of empty throne, an overturned goblet lying near, as though just drained. The* Queen *in seeming dazed, ecstatic state, raptly gazing upward and listening. Swarming forms and faces, in air above, seen eerily coming and going, blending and intermingling in domed ceiling-spaces of the court. Weird music. Mystic, luminous, beautiful faces detached from swarm, float, singly, forward, tremulously, and in succession, poising in mid-air and chanting.*

FIRST FACE.

And who hath known her—like as *I*
Have known her?—since the envying sky
Filched from her cheeks its morning-hue,
And from her eyes its glory, too,
Of dazzling shine and diamond dew.

SECOND FACE.

I knew her—long and long before
High Æo loosed her palm and thought:
"What awful splendor have I wrought
To dazzle earth and Heaven, too!"

THIRD FACE.

I knew her—long ere night was o'er—
Ere Æo yet conjectured what`
To fashion day of—aye, before
He sprinkled stars across the floor
Of night, and swept that form of mine,
E'en as a fleck of blinded shine,
Back to the black where light was not.

FOURTH FACE.

Ere day was dreamt, I saw her face
Lift from some starry hiding-place

Where our old moon was kneeling while
She lit its features with her smile.

FIFTH FACE.

I knew her while these islands yet
Were nestlings—ere they feathered wing,
Or e'en could gape with them, or get
Apoise the laziest-ambling breeze,
Or cheep, chirp out, or anything!·
When Time crooned rhymes of nurseries
Above them—nodded, dozed and slept,
And knew it not, till, wakening,
The morning stars began to sing,
And Heaven's first tender dews were wept.

SIXTH FACE.

I knew her when the jealous hands
Of Angels set her sculptured form
Upon a pedestal of storm
And let her to this land with strands
Of twisted lightnings.

SEVENTH FACE.

And I heard
Her voice ere she could tone a word

Of any but the Seraph-tongue.—
And O, sad-sweeter than all sung
Or word-said things !—to hear her say,
Between the tears she dashed away:—
" Lo, launched from the offended sight
Of Æo !—anguish infinite
Is ours, O Sisterhood of Sin !
Yet is thy service mine by right,
And sweet as I may rule it, thus
Shall Sin's myrrh-savor taste to us—
Sin's Empress—let my reign begin ! "

CHORUS OF SWARMING FACES.

We follow thee forever on !
Through darkest night and dimmest dawn ;
Through storm and calm—through shower and shine,
Hear thou our voices answering thine :
     We follow—*craving* but to be
     Thy followers.—We follow thee—
     We follow, follow, follow thee !

We follow ever on and on—
O'er hill and hollow, brake and lawn ;
Through gruesome vale and dread ravine
Where light of day is never seen.—

OF THE NIGHT.

We waver not in loyalty,—
Unfaltering we follow thee—
We follow, follow, follow thee!

We follow ever on and on!
The shroud of night around us drawn,
Though wet with mists, is wild-ashine
With stars that light that path of thine;—
The glowworms, too, befriend us—we
Shall fail not as we follow thee.
We follow, follow, follow thee!

We follow ever on and on.—
The notchéd reeds we pipe upon
Are pithed with music, keener blown
And blither where thou leadest lone—
Glad pangs of its ecstatic glee
Shall reach thee as we follow thee.
We follow, follow, follow thee!

We follow ever on and on:
We know the ways thy feet have gone,—
The grass is greener, and the bloom
Of roses richer in perfume—
And birds of every blooming tree
Sing sweeter as we follow thee.
We follow, follow, follow thee!

We follow ever on and on ;

For wheresoever thou hast gone

We hasten joyous, knowing there

Is sweeter sin than otherwhere—

  Leave still its latest cup, that we

  May drain it as we follow thee.

  We follow, follow, follow thee !

[*Throughout final stanzas, faces in fore-, and forms in back-ground, slowly vanish, and voices gradually fail to sheer silence.* CRESTILLOMEEM *rising, and wistfully gazing and listening; then, evidently regaining wonted self, looks to be assured of being utterly alone—then speaks.*]

CRESTILLOMEEM.

The Throne is throwing wide its gilded arms

To welcome me.   The Throne of Krung !   Ha ! ha !

Leap up, ye lazy echoes, and laugh loud !

For I, Crestillomeem, the Queen—ha ! ha !

Do fling my richest mirth into your mouths

That ye may fatten ripe with mockery !

I marvel what the kingdom would become

Were I not here to nurse it like a babe

And dandle it above the reach and clutch

Of intermeddlers in the royal line

And their attendant serfs. *Ho!* Jucklet, ho!
'Tis time my knarléd warp of nice anatomy
Were here, to weave us on upon our mesh
Of silken villainies. *Ho!* Jucklet, ho!

[*Lifts secret door in pave and drops a star-bud through the opening. Enter* JUCKLET *from below.*]

JUCKLET.

Spang sprit! my gracious Queen! but thou hast scorched
My left ear to a cinder! and my head
Rings like a ding-dong on the coast of death!
For, patient hate! thy hasty signal burst
Full in my face as hitherward I came!
But though my lug be fried to crisp, and my
Singed wig stinks like a little sun-stewed Wunk,
I stretch my fragrant presence at thy feet
And kiss thy sandal with a blistered lip.

CRESTILLOMEEM.

Hold! rare-done fool, lest I may bid the cook
To bake thee brown ! How fares the King by this?

JUCKLET.

I left him sleeping like a quinsied babe
Next the guest-chamber of a poor man's house:

But ere I came away to rest mine ears,
I salved his welded lids, uncorked his nose,
And o'er the odorous blossom of his lips
Re-squeezed the tinctured sponge, and felt his pulse
Come staggering back to regularity.
And four hours hence his Highness will awake
And Peace will take a nap!

CRESTILLOMEEM.

Ha! What mean you?

JUCKLET.   [*Ominously.*]

I mean that he suspects our knaveries.—
Some covert spy is burrowed in the court—
Nay, and I pray thee startle not *aloud*,
But mute thy very heart in its out-throb,
And let the blenching of thy cheeks but be
A whispering sort of pallor!

CRESTILLOMEEM.

A spy?—Here?

JUCKLET.

Aye, *here*—and haply even *now*.   And one
Whose unseen eye seems ever focused keen

Upon our action, and whose hungering ear
Eats every crumb of counsel that we drop
In these our secret interviews!—For he—
The King—through all his talking-sleep to-day
Hath jabbered of intrigue, conspiracy—
Of treachery and hate in fellowship,
With dire designs upon his royal bulk,
To oust it from the Throne.

CRESTILLOMEEM.

He spake my name?

JUCKLET.

O Queen, he speaks not ever but thy name
Makes melody of every sentence.—Yea,
He thinks thee even true to him as thou
Art fickle, false and subtle!   O how blind
And lame, and deaf and dumb, and worn and weak,
And faint, and sick, and all-commodious
His dear love is!

CRESTILLOMEEM.

Wilt thou wind up thy tongue,
Nor let it tangle in a knot of words!
What said the King?

2

JUCKLET.

He said: "Crestillomeem—
O that she knew this great distress of mine!
For she would counsel with me, and her voice
Would flow in limpid wisdom o'er my wounds,
And, like a love-balm, lave my secret grief
And lull my sleepless heart!"—And so went on,
Struggling all maudlin in the wrangled web
That well nigh hath cocooned him!

CRESTILLOMEEM.

Did he yield
No hint of this mysterious distress
He needs must hold sequestered from his Queen?
What said he in his talking-sleep by which
Some clue were gained of how and when and whence
His trouble came?

JUCKLET.

In one strange phase he spake
As though some sprited lady talked with him.—
Full courteously he said: "In woman's guise
Thou comest, yet I think thou art, in sooth,
But woman in thy form.—Thy words are strange

And leave me mystified.   I feel the truth
Of all thou hast declared, and yet so vague
And shadow-like thy meaning is to me,
I know not how to act to ward the blow
Thou sayest is hanging o'er me even now."
And then, with open hands held pleadingly,
He asked, "Who *is* my foe?"—And o'er his face
A sudden pallor flashed, like death itself,
As though, if answer had been given, it
Had fallen like a curse.

CRESTILLOMEEM.

I'll stake my soul
Thrice over in the grinning teeth of doom,
'Tis Dwainie of the Wunks who peeks and peers
With those fine eyes of hers in our affairs,
And carries Krung, in some disguise, these hints
Of our intent!   See thou that silence falls
Forever on her lips, and that the sight
She wastes upon our secret action blurs
With gray and grisly skum that shall for aye
Conceal us from her gaze while she writhes blind
And fangless as the fat worms of the grave!
Here! take this tuft of downy druze, and when

Thou comest on her, fronting full and fair,
Say "*Sherₜham!*" thrice, and fluff it in her face.

JUCKLET.

Thou knowest scanty magic, O my Queen,
But all thou dost is fairly excellent—
An *this* charm work, thou shalt have fuller faith
Than still I must withhold.
    [*Takes charm, with extravagant salutation.*]

CRESTILLOMEEM.

                Thou gibing knave!
Thou thing! Dost dare to name my sorcery
As any trifling gift? Behold what might
Be thine an thy deserving wavered not
In stable and abiding service to
Thy Queen! [*She presses suddenly her palm upon his eyes,
then lifts her softly-opening hand upward, his gaₜe following, where, slowly shaping in the air above them, appears the counter-self of* CRESTILLOMEEM, *clothed in
most radiant youth, her maiden-face bent downward to a
moonlit sward, where kneels a lover-knight, flawless in
manly symmetry and princely beauty,—yet none other than
the counterpart of* JUCKLET, *eerily and with strange
sweetness singing, to some curiously-tinkling instrument, the*

praises of its queenly mistress : JUCKLET *and* CRESTIL-
LOMEEM *transfixed below and trancedly gazing on their
mystic selves above.*]

SEMBLANCE OF JUCKLET—SINGS.

Crestillomeem !

   Crestillomeem !

Soul of my slumber !   Dream of my dream !

Moonlight may fall not as goldenly fair

As falls the gold of thine opulent hair—

Nay, nor the starlight as dazzlingly gleam

As gleam thine eyes, 'Meema—Crestillomeem !—

   Stars of the skies, 'Meema—

      Crestillomeem !

SEMBLANCE OF CRESTILLOMEEM—SINGS.

O Prince divine !

   O Prince divine !

Tempt thou me not with that sweet voice of thine !

Though my proud brow bear the blaze of a crown,

Lo, at thy feet must its glory bow down,

That from the dust thou mayest lift me to shine

Heaven'd in thy heart's rapture, O Prince divine !—

   Queen of thy love ever,

      O Prince divine !

SEMBLANCE OF JUCKLET—SINGS.

Crestillomeem !

  Crestillomeem !

Our life shall flow as a musical stream—

Windingly—placidly on shall it wend,

Marged with maʒhoora-bloom banks without end—

Word-birds shall call thee and dreamily scream,

" Where dost thou cruise, 'Meema—Crestillomeem ?

  Witheraway, 'Meema ?—

     Crestillomeem !"

DUO.

  [Vision and voices gradually failing away.]

Crestillomeem !

  Crestillomeem !

Soul of my slumber !   Dream of my dream ;

Star of Love's light, 'Meema—Crestillomeem !

  Crescent of Night, 'Meema !—

     Crestillomeem !

CRESTILLOMEEM.

  How now, thou clabber-brainéd spudge !—
Thou squelk !—thou—

JUCKLET.

       Nay, O Queen! contort me not
To more condenséd littleness than now
My shaméd frame incurreth on itself,
Seeing what might fare with it, didst *thou* will
 Kindly to nip it with thy magic *here*,
And leave it living in that form i' the air,
Forever pranking o'er the daisied sward
In wake of sandal-prints that dint the dews
As lightly as, in thy late maidenhood,
Thine own must needs have done in flighting from
The dread encroachments of the King.

CRESTILLOMEEM.

            Nay—peace!

JUCKLET.

So be it, O sweet Mystic.—But I crave
One service of thy magic yet.—*Amphine!*—
Breed me some special, damnéd philter for
Amphine—the *fair* Amphine!—to chuck it him,
Some serenade-tide, in a sodden slug
O' pastry, 'twixt the door-crack and a screech
O' rusty hinges.—Hey! Amphine the rare!—
And let me, too, elect his doom, O Queen!—

Listed against thee, he, too, doubtless hath
Been favored with an outline of our scheme,—
And I would kick my soul all over hell
If I might juggle his fine figure up
In such a shape as mine!

CRESTILLOMEEM.

                    Then this:—When thou
Canst come upon him bent above a flower,
Or any blooming thing, and thou, arear,
Shalt reach it first and, thwartwise, touch it fair,
And with thy knuckle flick him on the knee,—
Then—his fine form will shrink and shrivel up
As warty as a toad's—so hideous,
Thine own shall seem a marvel of rare grace!
Though idly speak'st thou of my mystic skill,
'Twas that which won the King for me: 'Twas that
Bereft him of his daughter ere we had
Been wedded yet a haed:—She strangely went
Astray one moonset from the palace-steps—
She went—nor yet returned.—Was it not strange?—
She would be wedded to an alien prince
The morrow midnight—to a prince whose sire
I once knew, in lost hours of lute and song,

When *he* was but a prince—*I* but a mouth
For him to lift up sippingly and drain
To lees most ultimate of stammering sobs
And maudlin wanderings of blinded breath.

JUCKLET. [*Aside.*]

Twigg-brebblets! but her Majesty hath speech
That doth bejuice all metaphor to drip
And spray and mist of sweetness!

CRESTILLOMEEM. [*Confusedly.*]

Where was I?
O, aye!—the princess went—she strangely went!—
E'en as I deemed her lover-princeling would
As strangely go, were she not soon restored.—
As so he did:—That airy penalty
The jocund Fates provide our love-lorn wights
In this glad island: So for thrice three nights
They spun the prince his line and marked him pay
It out (despite all warnings of his doom)
In fast and sleepless search for her—and *then*
They tripped his fumbling feet and he fell—UP!—
Up!—as 'tis writ—sheer past Heaven's flinching walls
And topmost cornices.—Up—up and on!—
And it is grimly guessed of those who thus

For such a term bemoan an absent love,
And so fall *upwise*, they must needs fall on—
And on and on—and on—and on—and on!
Ha! ha!

JUCKLET.

Quahh! but the prince's holden breath
Must ache his throat by this! But, O my Queen,
What of the princess?—and—

CRESTILLOMEEM.

The princess?—Aye—
The princess! Aye, she went—she strangely went!
And when the dainty vagrant came not back—
Both sire and son in apprehensive throes
Of royal grief—the very Throne befogged
In sighs and tears!—when all hope waned at last,
And all the spies of Spirkland, in her quest,
Came straggling empty-handed home again,—
Why, then the wise King sleeved his rainy eyes
And sagely thought the pretty princess had
Strayed to the island's edge and tumbled off.
I could have set his mind at ease on that.—
I could have told him, *yea*, she tumbled off—
I tumbled her!—and tumbled her so plump,

She tumbled in an under-island, then
Just slow-unmooring from our own and poised
For unknown voyagings of flight afar
And all remote of latitudes of ours.—
Aye, into that land I tumbled her, from which
But one charm known to art can tumble her
Back into this, and *that* charm, guilt be praised!
Is lodged not in the wit nor the desire
Of my rare lore.

                    JUCKLET.

              Thereinasmuch find joy!
But dost thou know that rumors flutter now
Among thy subjects of thy sorceries?—
The art being *banned*, thou knowest; or, unhoused,
Is unleashed pitilessly by the grim,
Facetious body of the dridular
Upon the one who fain had loosed the curse
On others.—An my counsel be worth ought,
Then have a care thy spells do not revert
Upon thyself, nor yet mine own poor hulk
O' fearsomeness!

              CRESTILLOMEEM.

              Ha! ha! No vaguest need
Of apprehension there!—While Krung remains—

[*She abruptly pauses—startled first, then listening curiously and with awed interest. Voice of exquisite melodiousness and fervor heard singing.*]

VOICE.

When kings are kings, and kings are men—
  And the lonesome rain is raining!—
O who shall rule from the red throne then,
And who shall covet the scepter when—
  When the winds are all complaining?

When men are men, and men are kings—
  And the lonesome rain is raining!—
O who shall list as the minstrel sings
Of the crown's fiat, or the signet-ring's,
  When the winds are all complaining?

CRESTILLOMEEM.

Whence flows such sweetness, and what voice is that?

JUCKLET.

The voice of Spraivoll, an mine ears be perked
And whetted o' late honied memories
Behaunting the deserted purlieus of
The court.

CRESTILLOMEEM.

And who is Spraivoll, and what song
Is that she sings so blinding exquisite
Of cadenced mystery?

JUCKLET.

Spraivoll—O Queen,—
Spraivoll the Tune-Fool is she called
By those who meet her ere the day long wanes
And naught but janiteering sparsely frets
The cushioned silences and stagnant dusts
Indifferently resuscitated by
The drowsy varlets in mock servitude
Of so refurbishing the royal halls:
She cometh, alien, from Wunkland—so
Hath she deposed to divers questioners
Who have been smitten of her voice—as rich
In melody as she is poor in caste and intellect.
She hath been roosting, pitied of the hinds
And scullions, round about the palace here
For half a node.

CRESTILLOMEEM.

And pray, where is she perched—
This wildbird-woman with her wondrous throat?

JUCKLET.

Under some dingy cornice, like enough—
Though *wildbird* she is not, being pluméd in,
Not feathers, but one fustioned stole—the like
Of which so shameth her fair face one needs
Must swear some lusty oaths, but that they shape
Themselves full gentlewise in mildest prayer :—
Not *wildbird ;*—nay, nor *woman*—though, in truth,
She is a licensed idiot, and drifts
About, as restless and as useless, too,
As any lazy breeze in summertime.
I 'll call her forth to greet your Majesty.
Ho! Spraivoll! Ho! my twittering birdster, flit
Thou hither.
[*Enter* SPRAIVOLL—*from behind group of statuary—singing.*]

SPRAIVOLL.

Ting-aling! Ling-ting! Tingle-tee!
The moon spins round and round for me!
Wind it up with a golden key.
Ting-aling! Ling-ting! Tingle-tee!

CRESTILLOMEEM.

Who art thou, and what the strange
Elusive beauty and intent of thy

Sweet song? What singest thou, vague, mystic-bird—
What doth the Tune-Fool sing? Aye, sing me what.

SPRAIVOLL. [*Singing.*]

What sings the breene on the wertling-vine,
   And the tweck on the bamner-stem?
Their song, to me, is the same as mine,
   As mine is the same to them—to them—
     As mine is the same to them.

In star-starved glooms where the plustre looms
   With its slender boughs above,
Their song sprays down with the fragrant blooms,—
   And the song they sing is love—is love—
     And the song they sing is love.

JUCKLET.

Your Majesty may be surprised somewhat,
But Spraivoll can not talk, her only mode
Of speech is melody; and thou mightst put
The dowered fool a thousand queries, and,
In like return, receive a thousand songs,
All set to differing tunes—as full of naught
As space is full of emptiness.

CRESTILLOMEEM.

                    A fool?—
And with a gift so all-divine!—A fool?

JUCKLET.

Aye, warranted!—The Flying Islands all
Might flock in mighty counsel—moult, and shake
Their loosened feathers, and sort every tuft,
Nor ever most minutely quarry there
One other Spraivoll, itching with her voice
Such favored spot of cuticle as she
Alone selects here in our blissful realm.

CRESTILLOMEEM.

Out, jester, on thy cumbrous wordiness!
Come hither, Tune-Fool, and be not afraid,
For I like fools so well I married one:
And since thou art a *Queen* of fools, and he
A *King*, why, I've a mind to bring you two
Together in some wise.   Canst use thy song
All times in such entrancing spirit, one
Who lists must so needs list, e'en though the song
Go on unceasingly indefinite?

SPRAIVOLL. [*Singing.*]

If one should ask me for a song,
  Then I should answer, and my tongue
Would twitter, trill and troll along
  Until the song were done.

Or should one ask me for my tongue,
  And I should answer with a song,
I 'd trill it till the song were sung,
  And troll it all along.

CRESTILLOMEEM.

Thou art indeed a fool, and one, I think,
To serve my present purposes. Give ear.—
And Jucklet, thou, go to the King and bide
His waking: then repeat these words :—" *The Queen*
Impatiently awaits his Majesty,
And craves his presence in the Tower of Stars,
That she may there express full tenderly
Her great solicitude." And *then*, end thus,—
" *So much she bade, and drooped her glowing face*
Deep in the showerings of her golden hair,
And with a flashing gesture of her arm
Turned all the moonlight pallid, saying, 'Haste ! ' "
  3

JUCKLET.

And would it not be well to hang a pearl
Or twain upon thy silken lashes?

CRESTILLOMEEM.

Go! [*Exit Jucklet.*]

Now, Tune-Fool, let me give thee topic for
A song: An Empress once, with angel in
Her face and devil in her heart, had wish
To breed confusion to her sovereign lord,
And work the downfall of his haughty son—
The issue of a former marriage—who
Bellowsed her hatred to the whitest heat,
For that her own son, by a former lord,
Was born a hideous dwarf, and reared aside
From the sire's knowing or his own—
That *none*, in sooth, might ever chance to guess
The hapless mother of the hapless child.
The Fiends that scar her thus, protect her still
With outward beauty of both face and form.—
It is so written, and must so remain
Till magic greater than their own is found
To hurl against her. So is she secure
And proof above all fear. Soh! listen well!—

Her present lord is haunted with a dream
That he is soon to die, and so prepares
(*All havoc hath been wrangled with the drugs!*)
The Throne for the ascension of the son,
His curséd heir, who still doth baffle all
Her arts against him, e'en as though he were
Protected by a skill beyond her own.
Soh ! she, the Queen, doth rule the King in all
Save this affectionate perversity
Of favor for the son whom he would raise
To his own place.—And but for this the King
Long since had tasted death and kissed his fate
As one might kiss a bride ! But so his Queen
Must needs withhold, not deal, the final blow,
She yet doth bind him, spelled, still trusting her ;
And, by her craft and wanton flatteries,
Doth sway his love to every purpose but
The one most coveted.—And for this end
She would make use of thee ;—and if thou dost
Her will, as her good pleasure shall direct,
Why, thou shalt sing at court, in silken tire,
Thy brow bound with wild diamonds, and thy hair
Sown with such gems as laugh hysteric lights
From glittering quespar, guenk and plennocynth,—

Aye, even panoplied as might the fair

Form of a very princess be, thy voice

Shall woo the echoes of the listening Throne.

SPRAIVOLL.   [*Crooning abstractedly.*]

And O! shall one—high brother of the air,

In deeps of space—shall he have dream as fair?—

And shall that dream be this?—In some strange place

Of long-lost lands he finds her waiting face—

Comes marveling upon it, unaware,

Set moonwise in the midnight of her hair,

And is behaunted with old nights of May,

So his glad lips do purl a roundelay

Purloinéd from the echo-triller's beak,

Seen keenly notching at some star's blanch cheek

With its ecstatic twitterings, through dusk

And sheen of dewy boughs of bloom and musk.

For him, Love, light again the eyes of her

That show nor tears, nor laughter, nor surprise—

For him undim their glamour and the blur

Of dreams drawn from the depths of deepest skies.

He doth not know if any lily blows

As fair of feature, nor of any rose.

CRESTILLOMEEM. [*Aside.*]

O this weird woman! she doth drug mine ears
With her uncanny sumptuousness of song!
[*To Spraivoll.*] Nay, nay! Give o'er thy tuneful maunder-
    ings
And mark me further, Tune-Fool—aye, and well:—
At present doth the King lie in a sleep
Drug-wrought and deep as death—the after-phase
Of an unconscious state, in which each act
Of his throughout his waking hours is so
Rehearsed, in manner, motion, deed and word,
Her spies (the Queen's) that watch him, serving there
As guardians o'er his royal slumbers, may
Inform her of her lord's most secret thought.
And lo, her plans have ripened even now
Till, *should he come upon his Throne to-night,*
Where eagerly his counselors will bide
His coming,—she, the Queen, hath reason to
Suspect her long-designéd purposes
May fall in jeopardy ;—but if he *fail*,
Through *any* means, to lend his presence there,—
Then, by a wheedled mandate, *is his Queen*
Empowered with all Sovereignty to reign
And work the royal purposes instead.

Therefore, the Queen hath set an interview—
A conference to be holden with the King,
Which is ordained to fall on noon to-night,
Twelve star-twirls ere the nick the Throne convenes.—
And with her thou shalt go, and bide in wait
Until she signal thee to sing ; and then
Shalt thou so work upon his mellow mood
With that unSpirkly magic of thy voice—
So all bedaze his waking thought with dreams,—
The Queen may, all unnoticed, slip away,
And leave thee singing to a throneless King.

SPRAIVOLL.   [*Singing.*]

And who shall sing for the haughty son
     While the good King droops his head?—
And will he dream, when the song is done,
     That a princess fair lies dead?

CRESTILLOMEEM.

The haughty son hath found *his* "Song"—*sweet curse!*—
And may she sing his everlasting dirge!
She comes from that near-floating land of thine,
Naming herself a princess of that realm
So strangely peopled we would fain evade
All mergence, and remain as strange to them

As they to us.   No less this Dwainie hath
Most sinuously writhed and lithed her way
Into court-favor here—hath glidden past
The King's encharméd sight and sleeked herself
Within the very altars of his house—
His line—his blood—his very life:—*AMPHINE!*
Not any Spirkland gentlemaiden might
Aspire so high as *she* hath dared to dare!—
For she, with her fair skin and finer ways,
And beauty second only to the Queen's,
Hath caught the Prince betwixt her mellow palms
And stroked him flutterless.   Didst ever thou
In thy land hear of *Dwainie of the Wunks?*

SPRAIVOLL.   [*Singing.*]

Ay, Dwainie!   My Dwainie!
        The lurloo ever sings,
A tremor in his flossy crest
        And in his glossy wings.
And Dwainie!—My Dwainie!
        The winno-welvers call;—
But Dwainie hides in Spirkland
        And answers not at all.

The teeper twitters Dwainie!—
   The tcheucker on his spray
Teeters up and down the wind
   And will not fly away:
And Dwainie!—My Dwainie!
   The drowsy oovers drawl;—
But Dwainie hides in Spirkland
   And answers not at all.

O Dwainie!—My Dwainie!
   The breezes hold their breath—
The stars are pale as blossoms,
   And the night as still as death:
And Dwainie!—My Dwainie!
   The fainting echoes fall;—
But Dwainie hides in Spirkland
   And answers not at all.

CRESTILLOMEEM.

A melody ecstatic! and thy words,
Although so meaningless, seem something more—
A vague and shadowy something, eerie-like,
That maketh one to shiver over-chilled
With curious, creeping sweetnesses of pain,

And catching breaths that flutter tremulous
With sighs that dry the throat out icily.—
But save thy music! Come! that I may make
Thee ready for thy royal auditor.   [*Exeunt.*]

END ACT 1.

ACT II.

SCENE II. *A garden of* KRUNG'S *Palace, screened from the moon with netted glenk-vines and blooming ʒhoomer-boughs, all glimmeringly lighted with star-flakes. An arbor, near which is a table spread with a repast—two seats, drawn either side. A playing fountain, at marge of which* AM-PHINE *sits thrumming a trentoraine.*

AMPHINE.   [*Improvising.*]

Ah, help me! but her face and brow
Are lovelier than lilies are
Beneath the light of moon and star
That smile as they are smiling now—
White lilies in a pallid swoon
Of sweetest white beneath the moon—
White lilies, in a flood of bright
Pure lucidness of liquid light
Cascading down some plenilune,
When all the azure overhead
Blooms like a dazzling daisy-bed.—
So luminous her face and brow,

The luster of their glory, shed
In memory, even, blinds me now.

[*Plaintively addressing instrument.*]

O warbling strand of silver, where, O where
Hast thou unraveled that sweet voice of thine
And left its silken murmurs quavering
In limp thrills of delight?   O golden wire,
Where hast thou spilled thy precious twinkerings?—
What thirsty ear hath drained thy melody,
And left me but a wild, delirious drop
To tincture all my soul with vain desire?

[*Improvising.*]

Her face—her brow—her hair unfurled!—
And O the oval chin below,
Carved, like a cunning cameo,
With one exquisite dimple, swirled
With swimming shine and shade, and whirled
The daintiest vortex poets know—
The sweetest whirlpool ever twirled
By Cupid's finger-tip,—and so,
The deadliest maelstrom in the world.

[*Pauses.—Enter* DWAINIE *unperceived.*]

AMPHINE.   [*Again addressing instrument.*]

O Trentoraine! how like an emptiéd vase
Thou art—whose clustering blooms of song have drooped
And faded, one by one, and fallen away,
And left to me but dry and tuneless stems,
And crisp and withered tendrils of a voice
Whose thrilling tone, now like a throttled sound,
Lies stifled, faint, and gasping all in vain
For utterance.

[*Again improvising.*]

And O mad wars of blinding blurs
And flashings of lance-blades of light,
Whet glitteringly athwart the sight
That dares confront those eyes of hers!
Let any dew-drop soak the hue
Of any violet through and through,
And then be colorless and dull,
Compared with eyes so beautiful!
I swear ye that her eyes be bright
As noonday, yet as dark as night—
As bright as be the burnished bars
Of rainbows set in sunny skies,
And yet as deep and dark, her eyes,
And lustrous black as blown-out stars.

[*Pauses*—DWAINIE *still unperceived, radiantly smiling and wafting kisses down from trellis-window above.*]

AMPHINE. [*Again to instrument.*]

O empty husk of song !
If deep within my heart the music thou
Hast stored away might find an issuance,
A fount of limpid laughter would leap up
And gurgle from my lips, and all the winds
Would revel with it, riotous with joy ;
And Dwainie, in her beauty, would lean o'er
The battlements of night, and, like the moon,
The glory of her face would light the world—
For I would sing of love.

DWAINIE.

And she would hear,—
And, reaching overhead among the stars,
Would scatter them like daisies at thy feet.

AMPHINE.

O voice, where art thou floating on the air?—
O Seraph-soul, where art thou hovering?

DWAINIE.

I hover in the zephyr of thy sighs,
And tremble lest thy love for me shall fail

To buoy me thus forever on the breath
Of such a dream as Heaven envies.

AMPHINE.

Ah!

[*Turning, discovers* DWAINIE—*she feigning still invisibility,
while he, with lifted eyes and wistful gaze, preludes with
instrument—then sings.*]

Linger, my Dwainie! Dwainie, lily-fair,
Stay yet thy step upon the casement-stair—
Poised be thy slipper-tip as is the tine
Of some still star.—Ah, Dwainie—Dwainie mine,
          Yet linger—linger there!

Thy face, O Dwainie, lily-pure and fair,
Gleams i' the dusk, as in thy dusky hair
The moony zhoomer glimmèrs, or the shine
Of thy swift smile.—Ah, Dwainie—Dwainie mine,
          Yet linger—linger there!

With lifted wrist, whereround the laughing air
Hath blown a mist of lawn and claspt it there,
Waft finger-thipt adieus that spray the wine
Of thy waste kisses to'rd me, Dwainie mine —
          Yet linger—linger there!

What unloosed splendor is there may compare
With thy hand's unfurled glory, anyvvhere?
What glint of dazzling dew or jewel fine
May mate thine eyes?—Ah, Dwainie—Dwainie mine!
   Yet linger—linger there!

My soul confronts thee: On thy brow and hair
It lays its tenderness like palms of prayer—
It touches sacredly those lips of thine
And swoons across thy spirit, Dwainie mine,
   The while thou lingerest there.

[*Drops trentoraine, and, with open arms, gazes yearningly
on* DWAINIE.]

    DWAINIE.
       O

Thy words do wing my being dovewise!

    AMPHINE.
       Then,

Thou lovest!—O my homing dove, veer down
And nestle in the warm home of my breast!
So empty are mine arms, so full my heart,
The one must hold thee, or the other burst.

  DWAINIE. [*Throwing herself in his embrace.*]

Æo's own hand methinks hath flung me here:
O hold me that He may not pluck me back.

AMPHINE.

So closely will I hold thee that not e'en
The hand of death shall separate us.

DWAINIE.

So

May sweet death find us, then, that, woven thus
In the corolla of a ripe caress,
We may drop lightly, like twin plustre-buds,
On Heaven's star-strewn lawn.

AMPHINE.

So do I pray.

But tell me, tender heart, an thou dost love,
Where hast thou loitered for so long?—for thou
Didst promise tryst here with me earlier by
Some several layodemes, which I have told
Full chafingly against my finger-tips
Till the full complement, save three, are ranged
Thy pitiless accusers, claiming, each,
So many as their joinéd number be
Shalt thou so many times lift up thy lips
For mine's most lingering forgiveness.
So, save thee, O my Sweet! and rest thee, I
Have ordered merl and viands to be brought

For our refreshment here, where, thus alone,
I may sip words with thee as well as wine.
Why hast thou kept me so athirst?—Why, I
Am jealous of the flattered solitudes
In which thou walkest.   [*They sit at table.*]

DWAINIE.

                    Nay, I will not tell,
Since, an I yielded, countless questions, like
In idlest worth, would waste our interview
In speculations vain.—Let this suffice:—
I stayed to talk with one whom, long ago,
I met and knew, and grew to love, forsooth,
In dreamy Wunkland.—Talked of mellow nights,
And long, long hours of golden olden times,
When girlish happiness locked hands with me
And we went spinning round, with naked feet
In swaths of bruiséd roses ankle-deep ;
When laughter rang unsilenced, unrebuked,
And prayers went unremembered, oozing clean
From the drowsed memory, as from the eyes
The pure, sweet mother-face that bent above
Glimmered and wavered, blurred, bent closer still
A timeless instant, like a shadowy flame,
    4

Then flickered tremulously o'er the brow,
And went out in a kiss.

AMPHINE. [*Kissing her.*]

Not like to *this!*

O blesséd lips whose kiss alone may be
Sweeter than their sweet speech!   Speak on, and say
Of what else talked thee and thy friend?

DWAINIE.

We talked

Of all the past, ah me! and all the friends
That now await my coming. And we talked
Of O so many things—so many things—
That I but blend them all with dreams of when,
With thy warm hand clasped close in this of mine,
We cross the floating bridge that soon again
Will span the all-unfathomable gulfs
Of nether air betwixt this isle of strife
And my most glorious realm of changeless peace,
Where summer night reigns ever and the moon
Hangs ever ripe and lush with radiance
Above a land where roses float on wings
And fan their fragrance out so lavishly
That Heaven hath hint of it, and oft therefrom

Sends down to us across the odorous seas
Strange argosies of interchanging bud
And blossom, spice and balm.—Sweet—sweet
Beyond all art and wit of uttering.

AMPHINE.

O Empress of my listening Soul, speak on,
And tell me all of that rare land of thine !—
For even though I reigned a peerless king
Within mine own, methinks I could fling down
My scepter, signet, crown and royal might,
And so fare down the thornéd path of life
If at its dwindling end my feet might touch
Upon the shores of such a land as thou
Dost paint for me—*thy* realm ! Tell on of it—
And tell me if thy sister-woman there
Is like to thee—Yet nay ! for if thou didst,
These eyes would lose all speech of sight
And call not back to thine their utter love.
But tell me of thy brothers.—Are they great,
And can they grapple Æo's arguments
Beyond our skill? or wrest a purpose from
The pink side of the moon at Darsten-tide?
Or cipher out the problem of blind stars,

That ever still do safely grope their way
Among the thronging constellations?

DWAINIE.
Aye!

Aye, they have leaped all earthland barriers
In mine own isle of wisdom-working Wunks:—
'Twas Wunkland's son that voyaged round the moon
And moored his barque within the molten bays
Of bubbling silver: And 'twas Wunkland's son
That talked with Mars—unbuckled Saturn's belt
And tightened it in squeezure of such facts
Therefrom as even he dare not disclose
In full till all his followers, as himself,
Have grown them wings, and gat them beaks and claws,
With plumage all bescienced to withstand
All tensest flames—glaze-throated, too, and lung'd
To swallow fiercest-spirted jets, and cores
Of embered and unquenchable white heat:
'Twas Wunkland's son that alchemized the dews,
And bred all colored grasses that he wist—
Divorced the airs and mists and caught the trick
Of azure-tinting earth as well as sky:
'Twas Wunkland's son that bent the rainbow straight
And walked it like a street, and so returned

To tell us it was made of hammered shine,
Inlaid with strips of selvedge from the sun,
And burnished with the rust of rotten stars:
'Twas Wunkland's son that comprehended first
All grosser things, and took our worlds apart
And oiled their works with theories that clicked
In glib articulation with the pulse
And palpitation of the systemed facts.—
And, circling ever round the farthest reach
Of the remotest welkin of all truths,
We stint not our investigations to
Our worlds only, but query still beyond.—
For now our goolores say, below these isles
A million million miles, are *other* worlds—
Not like to ours, but *round*, as bubbles are,
And, like them, ever reeling on through space,
And anchorless through all eternity;—
Not like to ours, for our isles, as they note,
Are living things that fly about at night,
And soar above and cling, throughout the day,
Like bats, beneath the bent sills of the skies:
And I myself have heard, at dawn of moon,
A liquid music filtered through my dreams,
As though 'twere myriads of sweet voices, pent

In some o'erhanging realm, had spilled themselves
In streams of melody that trickled through
The chinks and crannies of a crystal pave,
Until the wasted juice of harmony,
Slow-leaking o'er my senses, laved my soul
In ecstasy divine: And afferhaiks,
Who scour our coasts on missions for the King,
Declare our island's shape is like the zhibb's
When lolling in a trance upon the air,
With open wings upslant and motionless.
O such a land it is—so all complete
In all wise habitants, and knowledge, lore,
Arts, sciences, perfected government—
In kingly wisdom, worth and majesty—
So furnished forth in all things lovable,
O Amphine, love of mine, it lacks but thy
Sweet presence to make it a paradise?

                              [*Takes up trentoraine.*]

And shall I tell thee of the home that waits
For thy glad coming, Amphine?—Listen, then!

CHANT-RECITATIVE.

A palace veiled in a glimmering dusk;
  Warm breaths of a tropic air,
Drugged with the odorous marzhoo's musk
  And the sumptuous cyncotwaire—
Where the trembling hands of the lilwing's leaves
  The winds caress and fawn,
While the dreamy starlight idly weaves
  Designs for the damask lawn.

Densed in the depths of a dim eclipse
  Of palms, in a flowery space,
A fountain leaps from the marble lips
  Of a girl, with a golden vase
Held atip on a curving wrist,
  Drinking the drops that glance
Laughingly in the glittering mist
  Of her crystal utterance.

Archways looped o'er blooming walks
  That lead through gleaming halls;
And balconies where the word-bird talks
  To the tittering waterfalls:

And casements, gauzed with the filmy sheen
  Of a lace that sifts the sight
Through a ghost of bloom on the haunted screen
  That drips with the dews of light.

Weird, pale shapes of sculptured stone,—
  With marble nymphs agaze
Ever in fonts of amber, sown
  With seeds of gold, and sprays
Of emerald mosses, ever drowned,
  Where glimpses of shell and gem
Peer from the depths, as round and round
  The nautilus nods at them.

Faces blurred in a mazy dance,
  With a music wild and sweet,
Spinning the threads of the mad romance
  That tangles the waltzers' feet:
Twining arms, and warm, swift thrills
  That pulse to the melody,
Till the soul of the dancer dips and fills
  In the wells of ecstasy.

Eyes that melt in a quivering ore
   Of love, and the molten kiss
Jetted forth of the hearts that pour
   Their blood in the molds of bliss.—
Till, worn to a languor slumber-deep,
   The soul of the dreamer lifts
A silken sail on the gulfs of sleep,
   And into the darkness drifts.

[*The instrument falls from her hands*—AMPHINE, *in stress of
passionate delight, embraces her.*]

AMPHINE.

Thou art not all of earth, O angel one!
Nor do I far miswonder me an thou
Hast peered above the very walls of Heaven!
What hast thou seen there?—Didst on Æo bask
Thine eyes and clothe Him with new splendorings?
And strove He to fling back as bright a smile
As thine, the while He beckoned thee within?
And, tell me, didst thou meet an angel there
Alinger at the gates, nor entering
Till I, her brother, joined her?

DWAINIE.

Why, hast thou
A sister dead?—Truth, I have heard of one
Long lost to thee—not dead?

AMPHINE.

Of her I speak,—
And dead, although we know not certainly,
We moan us ever it must needs be death
Only could hold her from us such long term
Of changeless yearning for her glad return.
She strayed away from us long, long ago.—
O and our memories!—Her wondering eyes
That seemed as though they ever looked on things
We might not see—as haply so they did,—
For she went from us, all so suddenly—
· So strangely vanished, leaving never trace
Of her outgoing, that I oftimes think
Her rapt eyes fell along some certain path
Of special glory paven for her feet,
And fashioned of Æo's supreme desire
That she might bend her steps therein and so
Reach Him again, unseen of our mere eyes.
My sweet, sweet sister!—lost to brother—sire—

And, to *her* heart, one dearer than all else,—
Her *lover*—lost indeed!

DWAINIE.

    Nay, do not grieve
Thee thus, O loving heart! Thy sister yet
May come to thee in some glad way the Fates
Are fashioning the while thy teardrops fall!
So calm thee, while I speak of thine own self.—
For I have listened to a whistling bird
That pipes of waiting danger. Didst thou note
No strange behavior of thy sire of late?

AMPHINE.

Aye, he is silent, and he walks as one
In some fixed melancholy, or as one
Half waking.

DWAINIE.

    Aye! and doth he counsel not
With thee in any wise pertaining to
His ailings, or of matters looking toward
His future purposes, or his intents
Regarding thine own future fortunings
And his desires and interests therein?

What bearing hath he shown of late toward thee
By which thou mightst beframe some estimate
Of his mind's placid flow or turbulent?
And hath he not so spoken thee at times
Thou hast been 'wildered of his words, or grieved
Of his strange manner?

AMPHINE.

Once he stayed me on
The palace-stairs and whispered, " Lo, my son,
Thy young reign draweth nigh—prepare! "—So passed
And vanished as a wraith, so wan he was!

DWAINIE.

And didst thou never reason on this thing, .
Nor ask thyself what dims thy father's eye
And makes a brooding shadow of his form?

AMPHINE.

Why, there's a household rumor that he dreams
Death fareth ever at his side, and soon
Shall signal away.—But *Jucklet* saith
Crestillomeem hath said *the leeches* say
There is no cause for serious concern ;
And thus am I assured 'tis nothing more

Than childish fancy of mine aging sire,—

And so, as now, I laugh, full reverently,

And marvel, as I mark his shuffling gait,

And his bestrangered air and murmurous lips,

As by he glideth to and fro, ha! ha!

Ho! ho!—I laugh me many, many times—

Mind, thou, 'tis *reverently* I laugh—ha! ha!—

And wonder, as he glideth ghostly-wise,

If ever *I* shall waver as I walk,

And stumble o'er my beard, and knit my brows,

And o'er the dull mosaics of the pave

Play chequers with mine eyes! Ho! ho! Ah! ha!

DWAINIE. [*Aside.*]

How dare I tell him? Yet I must—I must!

AMPHINE.

Why, art *thou*, too, grown childish, that thou canst

Find thee waste pleasure talking to thyself,

And staring frowningly with eyes whose smiles

I need so much?
DWAINIE.

Nay, rather say, their tears,

Poor thoughtless Prince! [*Aside.*] (My magic even now

Forecasts his kingly sire's near happening

Of nameless hurt and ache and awful stress
Of agony supreme, when he shall stare
The stark truth in the face!)

AMPHINE.

What—what mean you?

DWAINIE.

What mean I but thy welfare?   Why, I mean,
One hour agone, the Queen, thy mother—

AMPHINE.
                                          Nay,
Say only "Queen"!

DWAINIE.

—The Queen, one hour agone—
As so I learned from source I need not say—
Sent message craving audience with the King
At noon to-night, within the Tower of Stars.—
Thou knowest, only brief space following
The time of her pent session thereso set
In secret with the King alone, *the Throne*
Is set, too, to convene; and that *the King*
Hath lent his seal unto a mandate that,
Should he withhold his presence there, the Queen
Shall be empowered to preside—to reign—

Solely endowed to work the royal will
In lieu of the good King. Now, therefore, I
Have been advised that she, the Queen, by craft
Connives to hold him absent purposely,
That she may claim the vacancy—for what
Covert design I know not, but I know
It augurs danger to you both, as to
The Throne s own perpetuity. [*Aside.*] (Again
My magic gives me vision terrible:—
The Sorceress' legions balk mine own.—The King
Still hers, yet wavering. O save the King,
Thou Æo!—Render him to us!)

AMPHINE.

I feel
Thou speakest truth: and yet how know you this?

DWAINIE.

Ask me not that; my lips are welded close.—
And, *more,*—since I have dared to speak, and thou
To listen,—Jucklet is accessory,
And even now is plotting for thy fall.
But, Passion of my Soul! think not of me,—
For nothing but sheer magic may avail
To work me harm; —but look thee to thyself!

For thou art blameless cause of all the hate
That rankleth in the bosom of the Queen.
So have thine eyes unslumbered ever, that
No step may steal behind thee—for in this
Unlooked-of way thine enemy will come:
This much I know, but for what fell intent
Dare not surmise.—*So look thee, night and day*
That none may skulk upon thee in this wise
Of dastardly attack. [*Aside.*] (Ha! Sorceress!
Thou palest, tossing wild and wantonly
The smothering golden tempest of thy hair.—
What! lying eyes! *ye* dare to utter *tears?*
Help! help! Yield us the King!)

AMPHINE.

And thou, O sweet!
How art thou guarded and what shield is thine
of safety?

DWAINIE.

Fear not thou for me at all.—
Possessed am I of wondrous sorcery—
. The gift of Holy Magi at my birth :—
Mine enemy must *front* me in assault
And must with mummery of speech assail,

And I will know him in first utterance—
And so may thus disarm him, though he be
A giant thrice in vasty form and force.   [*Singing heard.*]
But, list! what wandering minstrel cometh here
In the young night?

VOICE.—[*In distance—singing.*]

The drowsy eyes of the stars grow dim;
The wamboo roosts on the rainbow's rim,
   And the moon is a ghost of shine:
· *The soothing song of the crule is done,*
But the song of love is a soother one,
   And the song of love is mine.
Then, wake! O wáke!
For the sweet song's sake,
  Nor let my heart
With the morning break!

AMPHINE.

                Some serenader.   Hist!
What meaneth he so early, and what thus
Within the palace garden-close? Quick; here!
He neareth! Soh! Let us conceal ourselves
And mark his action, wholly unobserved.

       [AMPHINE *and* DWAINIE *enter bower.*]

5

VOICE.   [*Drawing nearer.*]

The mist of the morning, chill and gray,
Wraps the night in a shroud of spray ;
   The sun is a crimson blot :
The moon fades fast, and the stars take wing ;
The comet's tail is a fleeting thing—
   But the tale of love is not.
Then, wake! O wake!
For the sweet song's sake,
   Nor let my heart
With the morning break!
                     [*Enter* JUCKLET.]

JUCKLET.

Ho! ho! what will my dainty mistress say
When I shall stand knee-deep in the wet grass
Beneath her lattice, and with upturned eyes
And tongue out-lolling like the clapper of
A bell, outpour her *that ?*   I wonder now
If she will not put up her finger thus,
And say, "Hist! heart of mine! the angels call
To thee!"   Ho! ho!   Or will her blushing face
Light up her dim boudoir and, from her glass,
Flare back to her a flame upsprouting from
The hot-cored socket of a soul whose light

She thought long since had guttered out?—Ho! ho!
Or, haply, will she chastely bend above—
A parian phantom, with its head atip
And twinkling fingers dusting down the dews
That glitter on the tarapyzma vines
That riot round her casement—gathering
Lush blooms to pelt me with, while I below
All winkingly await the fragrant shower?
Ho! ho! how jolly is this thing of love!
But how much richer, rarer, jollier
Than all the loves is this rare love of mine!
Why, my sweet Princess doth not even dream
I *am* her lover,—for, to here confess,
I have a way of wooing all mine own
And waste scant speech in creamy compliment
And courtesies all gaumed with winy words.—
In sooth, I do not woo at all—I *win!*
How is it now the old duet doth glide
Itself full ripplingly adown the grooves
Of its quaint melody?—And whoso, by-
The-*bye*, or, by-the-*way*, or, *for the nonce*,
Or, eke ye, *peradventure*, ever durst
Render a duet singly but myself?

[*Singing—With grotesque mimicry of two voices.*]

JUCKLET'S DUET.

How is it you woo?—and now answer me true,—
　How is it you woo and you win?
Why, to answer you true,—the first thing you do
　Is to simply, my dearest—begin.

But how can I begin to woo or to win
　When I don't know a win from a woo?
Why, cover your chin with your fan or your fin,
　And I'll introduce them to you.

But what if it drew from my parents a view
　With my own in no manner akin?
No matter!—your view shall be first of the two,—
　So I hasten to usher them in.

Nay, stay!　Shall I grin at the woo or the win?
　And what will he do if I *do?*
Why, the woo will begin with " How pleasant it's been! "
　And the win with " Delighted with you! "

Then supposing he grew very dear to my view—
　I'm speaking, you know, of the win?
Why, then, you should do what he wanted you to,—
　And now is the time to begin.

The time to begin? O then usher him in—
    Let him say what he wants me to do.
He is here.—He's a twin of yourself,—I am "Win,"
    And you are, my darling, my " Woo ! "
        [*Capering and courtesying to feigned audience.*]

That song I call most sensible nonsense ;
And if the fair and peerless Dwainie were
But here, with that sweet voice of hers, to take
The part of " Woo," I'd be the happiest " Win "
On this side of futurity! Ho! ho!

DWAINIE.   [*Aside to* AMPHINE.]
What means he?

AMPHINE.

            Why, he means that throatless head
Of his needs further chucking down betwixt
His cloven shoulders!
        [*Starts forward—Dwainie detaining him.*]

DWAINIE.

            Nay, thou shalt not stir!
See! now the monster hath discovered our
Repast. Hold! Let us mark him further.

JUCKLET.   [*Archly eyeing viands.*]

                                        What!

A roasted wheffle and a toc-spiced whum,

Tricked with a larvey and a gherghgling's tail!—

And, sprit me! wine enough to swim them in!

Now I should like to put a question to

The *guests;* but as there *are* none, I direct

Mine interrogatory to the host.   [*Bowing to vacancy.*]

Am I behind-time?—Then I can but trust

My tardy coming may be overlooked

In my most active effort to regain

A gracious tolerance by service now:—

Directing rapt attention to the fact

That I have brought mine appetite along,

I can but feel, ho! ho! that further words

Would be a waste of speech.

   [*Sits at table—pours out wine, drinks and eats voraciously.*]

                          —There was a time

When I was rather backward in my ways

In courtly company (as though, forsooth,

I felt not, from my very birth, the swish

Of royal blood along my veins, though bred

Amongst the treacled scullions and the thralls

I shot from, like a cork, in youthful years,

Into court-favor by my wit's sheer stress

Of fomentation.—*Pah! the stench o' toil!*)

Aye, somehow, as I think, I 've all outgrown

That coarse, nice age, wherein one makes a meal

Of two estardles and a fork of soup.

Hey! sanaloo! Lest my starved stomach stand

Awe-stricken and aghast, with mouth agape

Before the rich profusion of this feast,

I lubricate it with a glass of merl

And coax it on to more familiar terms

Of fellowship with those delectables.

> [*Pours wine and holds up goblet with mock courtliness.*]

Mine host!—Thou of the viewless presence and

Hush-haunted lip :—Thy most imperial,

Etherial, and immaterial health!

Live till the sun dries up, and comb thy cares

With star-prongs till the comets fizzle out

And fade away and fail and are no more!

> [*Drinks and refills goblet.*]

And, if thou wilt permit me to observe,—

The gleaming shaft of spirit in this wine

Goes whistling to its mark, and full and fair

Zipps to the target-center of my soul!

Why, now am I the veriest gentleman

That ever buttered woman with a smile,
And let her melt and run and drip and ooze
All over and around a wanton heart!
And if my mistress bent above me now,
In all my hideous deformity,
I think she would look over, as it were,
The hump upon my back; and so forget
The kinks and knuckles of my crooked legs,
In this enchanting smile, she needs must leap,
Love-dazzled, and fall faint and fluttering
Within these yawning, all-devouring arms
Of mine! Ho! ho! And yet Crestillomeem
Would have me blight my dainty Dwainie with
This feather from the Devil's wing!—But I
Am far too full of craft to spoil the eyes
That yet shall pour their love like nectar out
Into mine own,—and I am far too deep
For royal wit to wade my purposes.

DWAINIE. [*To* AMPHINE.]

What can he mean?

AMPHINE. [*Chafing in suppressed frenzy.*]

                    Ha! to rush forward and
Tear out his tongue and slap it in his face!

DWAINIE. [*Aside.*]

Nay, nay! Hist what he saith!

JUCKLET.

How big a fool—

How all magnificent an idiot

Would I be to blight *her*—(my peerless one!—

My very soul's soul!) as Crestillomeem

Doth instigate me to, for *her* hate's sake—

And inward *jealousy*, as well, belike!—

Wouldst have my Dwainie blinded to my charms—

For charms, good sooth, were every several flaw

Of my malforméd outer-self, compared

With that his Handsomenes's, the Prince Amphine

Shall change to at a breath of my puff'd cheek,

E'en were it weedy-bearded at the time

With such a stubble as a huntsman well

Might lose his spaniel in! Ho! ho! Ho! ho!

I fear me, O my coy Crestillomeem,

Thine ancient coquetry doth challenge still

Thine own vain admiration overmuch!

I to crush *her* ?—when thou, as certainly,

Hast armed me to smite down the only bar

That lies betwixt her love and mine? Ho! ho!

Hey! but the revel I shall riot in

Above the beauteous Prince, instantuously

Made all abhorrent as a reptiled bulk!

Ho! ho! my princely wooer of the fair

Rare lady of mine own superior choice!

Pah! but my very 'maginings of him

Refinéd to that shaméd, sickening shape,

Do so beloathe me of him there be qualms

Expostulating in my forum now!

Ho! what unprincifying properties

Of medication hath her Majesty

Put in my tender charge! Ho! ho! Ho! ho!

Ah, Dwainie! sweetest sweet! what shock to thee!—

I wonder, when she sees the human toad

Squat at her feet and cock his filmy eyes

Upon her and croak love, if she will not

Call me to tweezer him with two long sticks

And toss him from her path.—O ho! Ho! ho!

Hell bend him o'er some blossom quick, that I

May have one brother in the flesh!

                               [*Nods drowsily.*]

DWAINIE. [*To* AMPHINE.]

                        Ha! See!

He groweth drunken.—Soh! Bide yet a spell

And I will vex him with my sorcery:
Then shall we hence, for lo, the node when all
Our subtlest arts and strategies must needs
Be quickened into acts and swift results.
Now bide thou here, and in mute silence mark
The righteous penalty that hath accrued
Upon that dwarféd monster.

[*She stands, still in concealment from the dwarf, her tense gaze
fixed upon him as though in mute and painful act of incan-
tation.*—JUCKLET *affected drowsily—yawns and mum-
bles incoherently—stretches, and gradually sinks at full
length on the sward.*—DWAINIE *moves forward*—AM-
PHINE, *following, is about to set foot contemptuously on
sleeper's breast, but is caught and held away by* DWAINIE,
*who imperiously waves him back, and still, in panto-
mime, commanding, bids him turn and hide his face*—AM-
PHINE *obeying as though unable to do otherwise.* DWAI-
NIE *then unbinds her hair, and throwing it all forward
covering her face and bending till it trails the ground, she
lifts to the knee her dress, and so walks backward in a
circle round the sleeping* JUCKLET, *crooning to herself
an incoherent song. Then pausing, letting fall her gown,
and rising to full stature, waves her hands above the sleeper's face, and runs to* AMPHINE, *who turns about and
gazes on her with new wonderment.*]

DWAINIE.　[*To* AMPHINE.]

Now shalt thou
Look on such scaith as thou hast never dreamed.

[*As she speaks, half averting her face as with melancholy apprehension, chorus of lugubrious voices heard chanting discordantly.*]

VOICES.

When the fat moon smiles,
　　　　And the comets kiss,
　　　　　　　And the elves of Spirkland flit,
The Whanghoo twunkers
　　　　A tune like this,
　　　　　　　And the nightmares champ the bitt.

[*As chorus dies away, a comet, freighted with weird shapes, dips from the night and trails near* JUCKLET'S *sleeping figure, while, with attendant goblin-forms, two* Nightmares, CREECH *and* GRITCHFANG, *alight.—The comet hisses, switches its tail and disappears, while the two goblins hover buzzingly o'er* JUCKLET, *who starts wide-eyed and stares fixedly at them, with horribly contorted features.*]

CREECH.　[*To* GRITCHFANG.]

Buzz!

　　　Buzz!

　　　　　Buzz!

　　　　　　　Buzz!

Flutter your wings like your grandmother does!

Tuck in your chin and wheel over and *whir-r-r*

Like a dickerbug fast in the web of the wuhrr!

Reel out your tongue, and untangle your toes,

And rattle your claws o'er the bridge of his nose;

Tickle his ears with your feathers and fuzz,

And keep up a hum like your grandmother does!

　　　[JUCKLET *moans and clutches at air convulsively.*]

AMPHINE.ʻ　[*Shuddering.*]

Most gruesome sight! See how the poor worm writhes!

How must he suffer!

DWAINIE.

　　　　　Aye, but good is meant—

A far voice sings it so.

GRITCHFANG.　[*To* CREECH.]

Let me dive deep in his nostraline caves,

And keep an eye out as to how he behaves:

Fasten him down while I put him to rack—

And don't let him flop from the flat of his back!

[*Shrinks to minute size, while goblin attendants pluck from shrubbery a great lily-shaped flower which they invert funnel-wise, with small end at sleeper's nostrils, hoisting* GRITCHFANG *in at top and jostling shape downward gradually from sight, and—removing flower,—voice of* GRITCH-FANG *continues gleefully from within sleeper's head.*]

Ho! I have bored through the floor of his brains,
And set them all writhing with torturous pains;
And I shriek out the prayer, as I whistle and whiz,
I may be the nightmare that my grandmother is!

[*Reappears, through reversal of flower-method, assuming former shape, crosses to* CREECH, *and, joining, the twain dance on sleeper's stomach in broken time to duo.*]

DUO.

Whing!
     Whang!
          So our ancestors sang!
And they guzzled hot blood and blew up with a *bang!—*
But they ever tenaciously clung to the rule
To only blow up in the hull of a fool—
To fizz and explode like a cast-iron toad
In the cavernous depths where his victuals were stowed—
When chances were ripest and thickest and best
To burst every button-hole out of his vest!

[*They pause, float high above, and fusing together into a great square iron weight, drop heavily on chest of sleeper, who moans piteously.*]

AMPHINE. [*Hiding his face.*]

Ah ! take me hence !

[DWAINIE *leads him off, looking backward as she goes and waving her hands imploringly to* CREECH *and* GRITCH-FANG, *reassuming former shapes, in ecstacies of insane delight.*]

CREECH. [*To* GRITCHFANG.]

Zipp !

Zipp !

Zipp !

Zipp !

Sting his tongue raw and unravel his lip !

Grope, on the right, down his windpipe, and squeeze

His liver as dry as a petrified wheeze !

[GRITCHFANG—*as before—shrinks and disappears at sleeper's mouth.*]

Throttle his heart till he's black in the face,

And bury it down in some desolate place

Where only remorse in pent agony lives

To dread the advice that your grandmother gives !

[*The sleeper struggles contortedly, while voice of* GRITCH-
FANG *calls from within.*]

GRITCHFANG.

Ho-ho ! I have clambered the rungs of his ribs
And be-riddled his lungs into tatters and dribs ;
And I turn up the tube of his heart like a hose
And squirt all the blood to the end of his nose !
I stamp on his stomach and caper and prance,
With my tail tossing round like a boomerang-lance !
And thus may success ever crown my intent
To wander the ways that my grandmother went !

[*Reappears, falls hysterically in* CREECH'S *outstretched arms.
—Then dance and chorus:*]

DUO.

Whing !
    Whung !
        So our ancestors sung !
And they snorted and pawed, and they hissed and they
    stung,—
Taking special terrific delight in their work
On the fools that they found in the lands of the Spirk.—
And each little grain of their powders of pain
They scraped up and pestled again and again—
Mixed in quadruple doses for gluttons and sots,
Till they strangled their dreams with gung-jibbrious knots !

[*The comet again trails past, upon which the* Nightmares *leap and disappear.* JUCKLET *staggers to his feet and glares frenziedly around—then starts for opposite exit of comet— is there suddenly confronted with fiend-faces in the air, bewhiskered with ragged purplish flames that flare audibly and huskily in abrupt alternating chill gasps and hot welterings of wind. He starts back from them, reels and falls prostrate, groveling terrifiedly in the dust, and chattering, with eerie music accompanying his broken utterance.*]

JUCKLET.

Æo! Æo! Æo!

Thou that dost all things know—

    Waiving all claims of mine to *dare* to pray,

Save that I needs *must* :—Lo,

    What *may* I pray for? Yea,

    I have not *any* way,

An *Thou* gainsayest me a tolerance so.—

    I dare not pray

      Forgiveness—too great

      My vast o'ertoppling weight

    Of sinning; nor can I

    Pray my

Poor soul unscourged to go.—

Frame *Thou* my prayer, Æo!

6

What may I pray for?   Dare
I shape a prayer,

     In sooth,

   For any canceled joy

    Of my mad youth,

  Or any bliss my sin's stress did destroy?

What may I pray for—What?—
That the wild clusters of forget-me-not

    And mignonette

    And violet

Be out of childhood brought,

   . And in mine old heart set

  A-blooming now as then?—

   With all their petals yet

Bediamoned with dews—
Their sweet, sweet scent let loose

   Full sumptuously again!

What *may* I pray, Æo!

   For the poor hutchéd cot

   Where death sate squat

Midst my first memories?—Lo!
My mother's face—(they, whispering, told me so)—

   That face!—so pinchedly

   It blanched up, as they lifted me—

Its frozen eyelids would

Not part, nor could

Be ever wetted open with warm tears.

. . . Who hears

The prayers for all dead-mother-sakes, Æo!

Leastwise *one* mercy:—May

I not have leave to pray

All *self* to pass away—

Forgetful of all needs

Mine own—

Neglectful of all creeds;—

Alone,

Stand fronting Thy high throne and say:

To Thee,

O Infinite, I pray

Shield *Thou* mine enemy!

[*Music throughout supplication gradually softens and sweetens into utter gentleness, with scene slow-fading into densest night.*]

END ACT II.

ACT III.

SCENE I.   *Court of* KRUNG—*Royal* Ministers, Counselors, *etc., in session.*   CRESTILLOMEEM, *in full blazonry
of regal attire, presiding.   She signals a* Herald *at her
left, who steps forward.*—*Blare of trumpets, greeted with
ominous murmurings within, blent with tumult from without.*

HERALD.

Hist, ho!   Ay, ay!   Ay, ay!—Her Majesty,

The All-Glorious and Ever-Gracious Queen,

Crestillomeem, to her most loyal, leal

And right devoted subjects, greeting sends—

Proclaiming, in the absence of the King,

Her royal presence—

[*Voice of* Herald *fails abruptly—utterly.*—*A breathless hush
falls sudden on the court*—*A sense oppressive—ominous*—
*affects the throng.   Weird music heard of unseen instru-
ments.*]

HERALD.   [*Huskily striving to be heard.*]

Hist, ho!   Ay, ay!   Ay, ay!—Her Majesty,

The All-Glorious and Ever-Gracious Queen,

Crestillomeem—

[*The* Queen *gasps, and clutches at* Herald, *mutely signing him to silence, her staring eyes fixed on a shadowy figure, mistily developing before her into wraith-like form and likeness of the Tune-Fool,* SPRAIVOLL. *The shape—evidently invisible and voiceless to all senses but the* Queen's *—wavers vaporishly to and fro before her, moaning and crooning in infinitely sweet-sad minor cadences a mystic song.*]

WRAITH-SONG OF SPRAIVOLL.

I will not hear the dying word
   Of any friend, nor stroke the wing
Of any little wounded bird.
   . . . Love is the deadest thing!

I wist not if I see the smile
   Of prince or wight, in court or lane.—
I only know that afterwhile
   He will not smile again.

The summer blossom, at my feet,
   Swims backward, drowning in the grass.—
I will not stay to name it sweet—
   Sink out! and let me pass!

I have no mind to feel the touch
*   Of gentle hands on brow and hair.—*
The lack of this once pained me much,
*   And so I have a care.*

Dead weeds, and husky-rustling leaves
*   That beat the dead boughs where ye cling,*
And old dead nests beneath the eaves—
*   Love is the.deadest thing!*

Ah! once I fared not all alone;
*   And once--no matter, rain or snow!—*
The stars of summer ever shone—
*   Because I loved him so!*

With always tremblings in his hands,
*   And always blushes unaware,*
And always ripples down the strands
*   Of his long yellow hair.*

I needs must weep a little space,
*   Remembering his laughing eyes*
And curving lip, and lifted face
*   Of rapture and surprise.*

O joy is dead in every part,
And life and hope ; and so I sing :
In all the graveyard of my heart
Love is the deadest thing !

[*With dying away of song, apparition of* SPRAIVOLL *slowly vanishes.* CRESTILLOMEEM *turns dazedly to throng, and with labored effort strives to reassume imperious air.— Signs for wine and tremulously drains goblet—sinks back in throne with feigned complacency, mutely waving* Herald *to proceed.*]

HERALD.   [*Mechanically.*]

Hist, ho !   Ay, ay !   Ay, ay !—Her Majesty,
The All-Glorious and Ever-Gracious Queen,
Crestillomeem, to her most loyal, leal
And right devoted subjects, greeting sends.
Proclaiming, in the absence of the King,
Her royal presence, as by him empowered
To sit and occupy, maintain and hold,
And therefrom rule the Throne, in sovereign state,
And work the royal will—[*Confusion.*] Hist, ho ! Ay, ay !
Ay, ay !—And be it known, the King, in view
Of his approaching dissolution—

[*Sensation among* Counselors, *etc., within, and wild tumult without and cries* "*Long live the* King!" *and* "*Treason!*" "*Intrigue!*" "*Sorcery!*"   CRESTILLOMEEM, *in suppressed ire, waving silence, and* Herald *striving to be heard.*]

HERALD.

Hist, ho! Ay, ay! Ay, ay!—The King, in view

Of his approaching dissolution, hath

Decreed this instrument—this royal scroll

> [*Unrolling and displaying scroll.*]

With royal seal thereunto set by Krung's

Most sacred act and sign—

[*General sensation within, and growing tumult without, with wrangling cries of* "*Plot!*" "*Treason!*" "*Conspiracy!*" *and* "*Down with the* Queen!" "*Down with the usurper!*" "*Down with the Sorceress!*"]

CRESTILLOMEEM.   [*Wildly.*]

Who dares to cry

"Conspiracy!" Bring me the traitor-knave!

[*Growing confusion without—sound of rioting.—Voice,* "*Let me be taken! Let me be taken!*" *Enter* Guards, *dragging* JUCKLET *forward, wild-eyed and hysterical—the* Queen's *gaze fastened on him wonderingly.*]

CRESTILLOMEEM.   [*To* Guards.]

Why bring ye Jucklet hither in this wise?

GUARD.

Because 'tis he who cries "Conspiracy!"
And who incites the mob without with cries
Of "Plot!" and "Treason!"

CRESTILLOMEEM. [*Starting.*]
                    Ha! Can this be true?
I 'll not believe it!—Jucklet is my fool,
But not so vast a fool that he would tempt
His gracious Sovereign's ire. [*To* Guards.] Let him be
     freed!
          [*Then to* JUCKLET, *with mock service.*]
Stand hither, O my Fool!

JUCKLET. [*To* Queen.]
                    What! I, thy fool?
Ho! ho! *Thy* fool?—ho! ho!—Why, *thou* art *mine!*
[*Confusion—Cries of "Strike down the traitor!"* JUCKLET—
     wrenching himself from grasp of officers.]
Back all of ye! I have not waded Hell
That I should fear your puny enmity!
Here will I give ye proof of all I say!
[*Presses toward throne, wedging his opposers left and right—*
     CRESTILLOMEEM *sits as though stricken speechless,*
     *waving him back—*JUCKLET, *fairly fronting her, with*
     folded arms, to throng continues.]

Lo! do I here defy her to lift up

Her voice and say that Jucklet speaks a lie.

[*At sign of* Queen, *officers, unperceived, close warily behind him.*]

And, further—I pronounce the document

That craven Herald there holds in his hand

A forgery—a trick—and dare the Queen,

Here in my listening presence, to command

Its utterance!

CRESTILLOMEEM.   [*Wildly rising.*]

Hold, hireling!   Traitor!—Fool!—

The Queen thou dost in thy mad boasts insult

Shall utter first thy doom!

[JUCKLET, *seized from behind by* Guards, *is hurled face upward on the dais at her feet, while a minion with drawn sword pressed close against his breast, stands over him.*]

—Ere we proceed

With graver matters, let this demon-knave

Be sent back home to hell.

[*With awful stress of ire, form quivering, eyes glittering and features twitched and ashen.*]

Give *me* the sword,—

The insult hath been mine—so even shall

The vengeance be?

[*As* CRESTILLOMEEM *seizes sword and bends forward to strike,* JUCKLET, *with superhuman effort, frees his hand, and, with a sudden motion and an incoherent muttering, flings object in his assailant's face,—* CRESTILLOMEEM *staggers backward, dropping sword, and with arms tossed aloft, shrieks, totters and falls prone upon the pave. In confusion following* JUCKLET *mysteriously vanishes; and as the bewildered* Courtiers *lift the fallen* Queen, *a clear, piercing voice of thrilling sweetness heard singing.*]

VOICE.

The pride of noon must wither soon—
    The dusk of death must fall;
Yet out of darkest night the moon
    Shall blossom over all!

[*For an instant a dense cloud envelopes empty throne—then gradually lifts, discovering therein* KRUNG *seated, in royal panoply and state, with* JUCKLET *in act of presenting scepter to him.—Blare of trumpets, and chorus of* Courtiers, Ministers, Heralds, *etc.*]

CHORUS.

    All hail! Long live the King!

KRUNG. [*To throng, with grave salutation.*]
Through Æo's own great providence, and through
The intervention of an angel whom

I long had deemed forever lost to me,

Once more thy favored Sovereign, do I greet

And tender ye my blessing, O most good

And faith-abiding subjects of my realm!

In common, too, with thy long-suffering King,

Have *ye* long suffered, blamelessly as he;

Now therefore, know ye all what, until late,

I knew not of myself, and with me share

The rapturous assurance that is mine,

That, for all time to come, are we restored

To the old glory and most regal pride

And opulence and splendor of our realm.

[*Turning with pained features to the strangely-stricken* Queen.]

There have been, as ye needs must know, strange spells

And wicked sorceries at work within

The very dais-boundaries of the Throne.

Lo! then, behold thy harrier and mine,

And with me grieve for the self-ruined Queen

Who grovels at my feet, blind, speechless, and

So stricken with a curse herself designed

Should light upon Hope's fairest minister.

[*Motions attendants, who lead away* CRESTILLOMEEM—
    The King *gazing after her, overmastered with stress of
    his emotions.—He leans heavily on throne, as though ob-*

livious to all surroundings, and shaping into speech his
varying thought, as in a trance, speaks as though witless
of both utterance and auditor.]

I loved her.—Why? I never knew.—Perhaps
Because her face was fair.—Perhaps because
Her eyes were blue and wore a weary air.
Perhaps! Perhaps because her limpid face
Was eddied with a restless tide, wherein
The dimples found no place to anchor and
Abide. Perhaps because her tresses beat
A froth of gold about her throat, and poured
In splendor to the feet that ever seemed
Afloat. Perhaps because of that wild way
Her sudden laughter overleapt propriety ;
Or—who will say,—perhaps the way she wept.
Ho!—have ye seen the swollen heart of summer
Tempest, o'er the plain, with throbs of thunder
Burst apart and drench the earth with rain? She
Wept like that.—And to recall, with one wild glance
Of memory, our last love-parting—tears
And all—It thrills and maddens me! And yet
My dreams will hold her, flushed from lifted brow
To finger-tips, with passion's ripest kisses
Crushed and mangled on her lips . . . O woman! while

Your face was fair, and heart was pure, and lips
Were true, and hope as golden as your hair,
I should have strangled you !

[*As* KRUNG, *ceasing to speak, piteously lifts his face,* SPRAI-
VOLL *all suddenly appears, in space left vacant by the*
Queen, *and kneeling and kissing the* King's *hand.—He
bends in tenderness, kissing her brow—then lifts and seats
her at his side.   Speaks then to throng.*]

                              Good Subjects—Lords :
Behold in this sweet woman here my child,
Whom, years agone, the cold, despicable
Crestillomeem—by baleful, wicked arts
And gruesome spells and fearsome witcheries,
Did spirit off to some strange otherland,
Where, happily, a Wunkland Princess found
Her, and undid the spell by sorcery
More potent—aye, *Divine*, since it works naught
But good—the gift of Æo, to right wrong.
This magic dower the Wunkland Princess hath
Enlisted in our restoration here,
In secret service, till this joyful hour
Of our complete deliverance.   Even thus.—
Lo, let the peerless Princess now appear !

[*He lifts scepter, and a gust of melody, divinely beautiful, sweeps through the court.—The star above the throne loosens and drops slowly downward, bursting like a bubble on the scepter-tip, and, issuing therefrom,* AMPHINE *and* DWAINIE, *hand-in-hand, kneel at the feet of* KRUNG, *who bends above them with his blessing, while* JUCKLET *capers wildly round the group.*]

JUCKLET.

Ho! ho! but I could shriek for very joy!
And though my recent rival, fair Amphine,
Doth even now bend o'er a blossom, I,
Besprit me! have no lingering desire
To meddle with it, though with but one eye
I slept the while she backward walked around
Me in the garden.

[AMPHINE *dubiously smiles*—JUCKLET *blinks and leers—*
and DWAINIE *bites her finger.*]

KRUNG.

Peace! good Jucklet! Peace!
For this is not a time for any jest.—
Though the old order of our realm hath been
Restored, and though restored my very life—
Though I have found a daughter,—I have lost

A son—for Dwainie, with her sorcery,
Will, on the morrow, carry him away.
'Tis Æo's largess, as our love is His,
And our abiding trust and gratefulness.

THE END.